MEMORIES OF TIME TRAVEL

A COLLECTION OF POEMS AND SHORT STORIES

NICK HORGAN

TSL Publications

First published in Great Britain in 2022
By TSL Publications, Rickmansworth

Copyright © 2022 Nick Horgan
Cover by Nick Horgan

ISBN / 978-1-914245-73-2

CONTENTS

SHORT STORIES / Prose

INTRODUCTION

Firstly, thank you for picking up this book, I hope it gives you something in return, every time.

A few things have changed since my first collection in 2017. There's more light-hearted writing, and more abstract writing, more nostalgia, and more doom and gloom, inevitable really considering the circumstances.

It's been easier to let the ideas percolate, let them build, let my subconscious work out the logic, as well as brainstorming around ideas to fill them out.

Prose particularly has been greatly helped by learning to not rush a scene, to stop treating all plot as problem solving. I've been helped through writing exercises designed to open up ideas rather than generate new ideas. And to listen to the idea.

But as before, many ideas have come from responding to the challenges of others, which opens new avenues, and avoids treading the same paths, and my own automatic responses.

And ideas have come from circumstances, from experiences, from searching for truth, and beauty, and mechanisms and motivations.

Thank you again to everyone at Pinner Writers Group, to everyone who attended sessions, shared work, or gave feedback, and to Nancy Stephenson for her workshops, and again to the writers who participated, and to all the readers and listeners at open mic nights in Pinner. It's all valuable and builds up confidence and belief and whatever it is that is needed to keep the pen moving.

Some of the pieces were topical when conceived and I hope they stand the test of time, with a few about the dark days of the pandemic, which should be easy to identify. At times I found it difficult to write during lockdown. It seemed such a waste, and was hard to be inspired when the future was so unclear and depressing, which was the same for other activities and plans. The pandemic changed everything for quite a while.

Some pieces are actually quite old in their inception, revived from ideas concealed in finished notebooks, some of which I couldn't imagine I'd written yet there they were, in my handwriting.

And mixed in is inspiration from other poems, songs, songwriters and artists, activists and truth-tellers.

THE TITLE

I've been thinking about how we make decisions and how that affects our lives, and what the future will look like, as a consequence of things we have already done.

Several pieces are directly about time travel (Out of Order, Ten Things, Unwinding History). And anything nostalgic is in a sense time-travel, back to that time, that phase of time. And any 'looking forward' is also time travel, to a place that doesn't exist except in our imaginations. So I've been running up and down the escalator of time, as it were, as it continues forward.

If we stay in the now, we are travelling with time, at the speed of time. And if we stay in the same moment, refusing to move with the times, time appears to be sending us backwards into the past, as we step backwards at the speed of time to relive those moments forever.

Or to use a different analogy, every decision we make adjusts the course of our life, some barely noticeable and some very significantly, meanwhile, while we are busy setting our course we don't know what is over the horizon.

Popular films have shown us the problems time travel causes, especially going backwards. Can you change the past, and get back to the present you know? Can you do it without causing other changes, the effects of which you have no knowledge of how they will play out.

Some changes would wipe out your future existence, does that make you a time orphan, or do you just parachute into the present with no back story, creating an empty slipstream in the immediate past?

And does any of this affect your memory, will you remember things that now cannot happen?

All this before I start on parallel universes.

So if I've gone back in time bringing the past to the present, or forward bringing the future into the now, thank you for time travelling with me.

It's only natural for a race concerned with cause and effect, regret and renewal, to be drawn to the ideas of erasing the past, or correcting the future, and recording what we've been through. Ultimately time travel (at present) is only possible within creativity, as we have been made temporal, mortal and accountable to time, yet also spiritual and redeemable by the creator of time.

One thing we do know, time knows the way forward.

NOTES

POEMS

THE OWL HOURS

Are you up with the larks or are you a night owl? A poem about staring into the night.

NOW THE FIRST HAVE FALLEN

This was written for and performed at A Day to Remember on Sunday 11th November 2018 as part of Harrow Arts Centre's Lest We Forget Season, to commemorate the centenary of Armistice Day. In some towns and villages nearly all the eligible men signed up and would have fought alongside each other, potentially decimating the male population of those places.

REMINISCE 1918

This was adapted from an earlier version of Reminisce, again for the centenary of Armistice Day, 11th November 2018.

ZONE 6 TO ZONE 4
(SEASONAL VARIATIONS MAY OCCUR)

A 12 minute tube journey on the Metropolitan line, I've made thousands of time, and yet once I started to take note it was less familiar than I remembered.

IF YOU WERE HERE

Thank you to Peter Keeble who suggested I cut off an extraneous explanation that was at the end of this piece.

MY FINEST HOUR

A local paper has a monthly poetry competition. The title that month was 'My Finest Hour' and the only rule was no more than 20 lines. This was my entry, which didn't win but got a mention in the next edition.

AT THE END OF THE EARTH

I spent some time at the climate protests in October (2019) in London, and in the evenings I'd see an almost completely different protest in the media, from the view of the police, or the commuter, or the taxi driver, but rarely from the view of the protesters or the planet, which was not great. Boris was laughing it off as uncooperative crusties when mostly it was the older middle aged (silver hair and walking boots), grandparents, parents, scientists and students, using their privilege where others couldn't. I was proud of the police being there (although there seemed to be an excessive number) to protect the protests as well as break them down, and the freedom there was to take the lead in raising awareness that month, that does not exist in other countries. There was an immense feeling of positivity and togetherness and sense, calmness peacefulness love and concern for our global neighbours, dare I say spirituality, and it was spreading. But the power is with the powerful and they have other concerns. This poem was written in the pessimism that followed. I'll be happy to be proved wrong in the future.

STORY OF TREES

As I approached a milestone date, with several good friends who go back a long way, I wrote this, the last poem before the pandemic hit.

THE DESCENT

Sometimes you crash, and you have to live only in the present for a while.

THE DIFFERENCE BETWEEN MEN AND WOMEN IN SHOES

A light-hearted poem about shoes (and stereotypes that might be true), the first of our writers group poetry challenge (shoes).

BLOOD IS RED

Another poetry challenge (blood). Tragic events highlighting that Black Lives didn't seem to Matter had taken place around a month previous.

AFTERGLOW

The final poetry challenge (wine). Maybe it's not all as it seems, or maybe it is.

WAITING IN THE DARK

At the time there had been a lot of waiting going on, waiting for a vaccine, waiting to see if Christmas would be locked down, waiting for a grown up in the White House, just waiting for things to get better,

MOMENT OF RECOGNITION

This came from several sources, the memory of a conversation long ago when I inarticulately described how music worked for me, crossed paths with a writing exercise about what makes life worth living, and there it was, popped out more or less fully formed in 5 minutes . . . if only it was always that easy. To be fair the ideas had been percolating in my memory for a while, I just needed the right angle to pour.

MOVING BACK IN

It was noticeable there was a bit more wildlife about during lockdown, or a bit less cautious. I wrote this for a wellbeing project/competition at work, it was placed.

WHO YOU DO NOT RECOGNISE
Conspiracy, estrangement, dementia – you decide.

FLOATING FREE
One needs to let go, to be free. And trust the one who holds you buoyant.

BEFORE
A poem about old friends, who we sometimes lose touch with, and sometimes regain, finding we'd never really lost them after all.

MACHINERY OF PRODUCTION
This was written in response to a poem on the transition from Winter to Spring by my aunt Clare Horgan, taking on the transition from Spring through Summer.

TEN THINGS FOUND IN A TIME TRAVELLER'S BACKPACK
Inspired by *Ten Things Found in a Shipwrecked Sailor's Pocket* by Ian MacMillan.

TAKE A MOMENT – CAROLS 2021
This was written for and read at a Christmas Carol Service.

BOY SOLDIER
Initially inspired by reports of the life of Kenji Goto, a Japanese journalist, murdered in Syria in 2015.

FENCES
It's not just about refugees.

HOLDING ON TO NOTHING
A song of sorts, about believing or trusting in the wrong things.

THE GLORIOUS RESTRUCTURE

Who doesn't love competing with their colleagues for their own job, with a wider reach of responsibilities, all because some more important people made short-sighted decisions resulting in far reaching cuts and redundancies. Of course I don't still feel like this, but you might.

MAYAKOVSKY SWAGGERY

He was a bit mad to say the least. He'd have something to say, and with the necessary swagger.

UNWINDING HISTORY
(OR IF I COULD TURN BACK CHER)

More time travel. If Cher could turn back time (or Michael J Fox, which dates me) what would she do differently? Maybe after a while Cher would realise the guy wasn't worth undoing time to undo a cruelty that she knows she wants to redo. How far back do we go and will it just mean different evils and atrocities?

GHOSTS

Dedicated to Tim Carter, who is still missed, we wish you well in your new circumstances; and to the camaraderie of team sports.

ARC OF THE DIVERS

I've found that people, especially those who like sport, can get quite into some of the 'minor' sports during the Olympics (hockey, archery, the keirin?). For me it's the diving, particularly the synchronised diving pairs. It's the grace, the speed and the neat entry, and the slow-motion replays.

MEMORIES AND SECRETS

This is an old one, that has taken decades to finish, although I suspect it will never be finally finished and will always be a work in progress. When you're young, and if you can stay young, there is always danger, originality, first discoveries, imagination and dreams in your heart for the future to deal with, and occasionally literal cliff edges, beauty, deep blue waters and places to escape to.

SHORT STORIES / PROSE

OUT OF ORDER
The first piece I wrote after my first book was published, from a title prompt. A bit of time travel confusion.

PLEASE LET IT BE SO
This also appears in the anthology *Where HUMAN RIGHTS and MENTAL HEALTH Interact* published by TSL Publications. Hopefully sometime in the near future conversations like this will be possible, because action will have been taken.

LAST CHANCE SALOON
This was written for the Australian Writers Centre's monthly competition 'Furious Fiction'. 500 words, in 55 hours, with certain words, items etc required in the story. An idea came to me, I worked it through in my head, by which time there was only time to write it down, sleep and redraft by the 1pm deadline.

THE INCONVENIENT ALIBI
Entered into the Pinner Writers Short Story Competition. Wasn't placed. Rewritten. Too much *Death in Paradise* and those convoluted red herrings was the inspiration.

SEVEN DWARVES
Seven separate stories in 30 words or less. One was written for a competition, the other six followed.

AFTER THE STORM
Not based on actual events (yet). This has a beginning and an end, you'll have to write the middle yourself.

POEMS

THE OWL HOURS

Ceasefire ends the restless day,
darkness descends, the blanket thickening
softening everything, impermanently.

The moon keeps a respectful distance,
after the all-pervading sun.
while the impatient world is sleeping,
dreaming of trouble tomorrow.

The calming dark.
the friendly night,
the gentle hum of the distance,
few hours of peace,
unhurried reflection.

Every noise hushed by its maker,
every light dimmed by its isolation,
every thought allowed to stretch and contract and settle.
Every breath at peace,
contemplating infinity, eternity, immortality

Memories emerge, holding hands,
they dance and sing, and wander off safe into the night.

And I will join them,
once I give in,
and close my eyes.

TIPPING POINT

I'm the tipping point on the rollercoaster of the day,
perched at the point of balance, a.m. to p.m.,
before the brakeless acceleration to the foot of the clock.
I'm a top o' the mornin' reminder,
that there's still time to get something done by lunch.

You know me,
the solution to is it 12 a.m. or 12 p.m.?
But you rarely notice me pass, my daily moment in time,
I'm 'the early one, the sensible one',
too early for drinks – let's keep it civilised,
too early to eat – what? – no breakfast?

No, no one has serenaded in the .. , noon hour
Or waited in second-hand-fixated anticipation, at two min-
   utes to . . . noon
they don't even scan.
But the hour of reckoning,
when a man finds out who he is,
when he's outnumbered and outgunned,
that's mine, that's what gets me high.

So, I lack the bad-boy glamour of the other twelve o'clock,
that dark lord of the night – ha !
You do realise he's on the clock,
Sober while his moment passes,
handing the baton to that dullard mid-day, in their endless
   relay.
"Midday to you my good fellow",
I mock him as I leave.
With my 24 hour pass, un-chaperoned.

No one to answer to, no direct antonym,
to loop the loop with, not in this language,
all alone,
So how do I spend this unfettered freedom?
Well, in the middle of the night I could be street racing,
    freebasing,
all kinds of nocturnal debauchery, secrets, saucery,
your expectations in reverse,
or maybe sat in bed, rhyming terrible verse,
        did I give myself away?

One day, I won't return,
retired by the grammar police,
pensioned-off to a beach in Acapulco,
Where I'll swim by the light of the silver moon,
'Til then, I'm perched on the tipping point,
where the clock strikes twelve, noon

ΠOW THE FIRST HAVE FALLEΠ

Outside daffodils heralded spring,
the crocuses had been and gone,
replaced by egg-yolk yellow and nature's clean white,
waving gently in the slight breeze,
the sun was shining,
leaving cool shadows slanting from one gravestone to the
  next,

On the surrounding hillsides, new calves raised their heads
curiously above the barbed wire,
and crows and gulls screeched at each other from the tops
  of trees,

It was warm for black coats but many were worn, out of
  respect,
black ties, black veils, black shadows under eyes,
it seemed the whole village had decided these boys
  deserved some symbolic attendance,
no matter how vague the acquaintance,
how long since crossing the threshold of a church.

Small boys fell in step once through the entrance gate,
their mothers glassy-eyed and silent, clutching daughters,
their fathers walked tall,
as if their dignity might be the last memory added to the
  young men's lives,
something the coffins could carry to the next destination

And hanging in the air was an unspoken fear,
an unavoidable line of thought,
present like a storm cloud over that bright warm spring
  day,

There would be more many more, now the first had fallen,
many more from that line of boys who'd signed up and
   shipped out,

The bullets and the gas and the bombs and the war had now
   reached even here,
this isolated pocket, this outpost was overrun,

And while it felt like the only place on earth to be shrouded
   in grief,
for surely this sharp emptiness was rare on a day like to-
   day,
Tomorrow's papers would tell again, of this same scene,
replicated across the river, and down the valley,
throughout the country, across the continent and beyond.

There would be more, many more days like these,
to bury the dead, and grieve their passing,
so many more,
for a generation scythed down in such numbers that we
   should never forget,
that surely this was the war to end all wars.

REMINISCE 1918

That's the last photo
– your proud uniform, your shy face.

Close the album shut, and hope to always remember you -

. . . the last words you wrote to me
. . . last meal we shared
. . . the last dance together, to the last song, we heard together
the last time we were both whole,

There'll be nothing more,
no more never befores,
never again.
The well is dry,
the leaves have fallen,
the stars are out,
our book is closed.

SILENCE

At first we talked because we wanted to
but talking became less as we grew comfortable
the quiet, a thin surface
vulnerable to disruption,

we waited, quietly, whispered occasionally, waited
no longer embarrassed at not speaking
and the quiet thickened and we let it peg us down,
let childish concerns sleep
while we seek peace,

the silence becoming part of us
drawing us into ourselves
comfortably, discovering,

the sound of the outside rushing by, dimmed
the movements of the wind, grew feint
the working of our bodies, still
and the curtain was drawn on nature's harmonies,

comfortable with quiet between us
we withdrew to our own silence, each
some journeys must be took alone
else there will be no story, to tell oneself,

for the silence we each seek is different
our silences, are the absence, of different things,

until silence
like still blood,

like the intake of a breath you cannot take
confronted with wonder, shock, loss, beauty
the gravity of an atomic explosion
muted by distance,

a knowing of ourselves, we allowed
no echoes, no marks of time
all is still
as silent as the sun
just the movement of water within water
felt not heard, the amplified silence of heavy snow,

this is not the silence of claustrophobic fear
of the bullet before the shot
the empty stare of the dark
at the bottom of the well
not a silence forced by detention, descent
with foreboding and judgement to come,

but a silence in the wealth of life
the healing of peace
like the moment before the event itself
the silence at the end of anticipation
before the baton twitches,
before the starter fires,
before the lights blaze bright
silence extended, in dwelt, and waited on,

so quiet and listen
let go all
still and listen
accepting the silence
the silence accepting us,

and there we sat each of us
until the silence let us go,

returning to a muted life
just a few favourite sounds, at first
the silence still present, woven in
and slowly with care
we threaded in voices
instruments of music and noise
at our own mindful speed
we threaded these back in
to the new patterns of our rearranged soul.

ZONE 6 TO ZONE 4

(SEASONAL VARIATIONS MAY OCCUR)

Waiting on the platform,
a journey I have taken thousands of times,
a spot near the rear
that lines up doors opening here
with first to the stairs there,
oily rainbow flashes on the rails
tell of the squeal of metal on metal,

then the sound rushing in,
the full locomotive cacophony
of roaring and screeching and clunking,
it thunders and rattles and chunters,
squeals and whistles to a stop,

the familiar sound of doors beeping and sliding
invites us in,
I step over the gap, and enter the tin can worm,
the iron tunnel of light, the mansize metal bendy straw,
cloudy eyes have already logged,
a front facing seat, with no neighbours,
and a voice, friendly yet authoritative,
announces where this is, where the next stop is
and where it all ends,
this announcement will advance with us,
adjusted at each stop,

doors beep and shut, we avert out eyes
from the rushers and leapers
and those too-late pretending they'd prefer the next train,

no one speaks,
except to those they brought for this purpose,
we don't have the energy for small talk,
everything I believe
would be a pleasure to share,
but small talk is a careful dance,
I don't want to remember the steps nor tread on toes,

we roll out picking up a smooth whining speed,
past a herringbone pattern of parked cars
gleaming like polished cobbles in the rain
hundreds of thousands of pounds of technology, idling,

all we have time for
is to daydream our journey away,
by book, phone, tablet, whatever, or
staring out of the window at the inhabited world,
the streets alive with cars and people,
the houses silent, empty or confining,

the wide expanse running alongside tapers
into a tunnel of green,
and under a bridge I used to live over,
emerging high above the roofline, as the road dips low
to overlook backs of houses, extensions and trampolines,

ahead the bridge reminds me of Brooklyn, briefly,
its striped shadows flicker,

the line of the high street swings towards us,
somewhere near the top, my home indistinguishable,
gone before I can put myself at my own front door,
the road rises to meet us again,
as we cut without heed through local contours,

the park on one side, and the hill I know so well,
then into another tunnel of green, slowing in the darkness,
a smooth glide to a stop, and a high pitched whistle,
it sounds quite different from the inside,

another announcement breaks the noisy silence,
look up for familiar faces,
award winning flower beds
abandoned to shades of green, and brown,
people enter in animated, and settle their vigour drained,

we pick up speed and the yellow safety lines lose definition,
bind weed covers wire fences like camouflage netting,

feel the difference between what is close and fast,
and what is distant and slow

The trees and leaves blur with speed,
my eyes drop to the cables running along the track,
they jump and flicker,
wobble and vibrate, racing with the train,
my eyes drawing an imaginary thread
from where I came,

bridges slow flash their shadows from overhead,

an immobile sky, dried white tyre tracks today,
the world might be upside down
and we are hanging,

sealed in this capsule
I can't put my hand out, to feel it all go by,

we emerge high above a busy high street,
a concrete battleship slides towards us,
dry docked, with the next shift,
lush overgrown shrubs knit a foliage fence,

the outside is let in, the doors beep and slide
new faces enter, fill gaps in the seats and settle,
the announcements are white noise, soon over,

we slide out past a coffee bar on one platform,
a Pisa of paint pots behind glass on the other,

behind a wall, high speed trains thunder through,
their passengers serene,

dark shadows of concrete,
make a sandwich of cars and light,
and a high sided wall pushes houses back from the tracks,
marked with sparse graffiti tags,

the view is shielded by overlapping green,
a missing piece in a jigsaw of trees
reveals the square lines of a school,

clang ! socked by an oncoming train
and rattled to the last of its carriages,

bare stumps of butchered trees,
executed without trial,
and gardens in all their variations,

manicured, evergreen, bare,
and abandoned trampolines,
tricycles and plastic slides,
our train hisses to a stop, no steam,

a bleaker station, isolated high above the gardens,
a black fence of metal rods and climbing bind weed,
flowers like gramophone speakers announce themselves,

we glide above the silent film playing on both sides,
slicing a slope between north and south,

the cables are still running with us,
and the tracks too,
their movement different,
a shift away a shift towards,
shimmering like swords,

to the south houses open up for the art deco garage,
unchanged in memory,
and a long triangle of allotments nestles between here,
and the other line coming in slowly,

we slow and slide then crawl next to empty tracks,
rails ablaze with red stemmed weeds,
while buses wait outside patiently,

one last set of announcements,
bleeps and sliding doors,
and we step onto the island, funnel up the stairs,
and separate out into our lives.

IF YOU WERE HERE

If you were here, in this room, right in front of me,
I would say,
stand close,
so I can lay my hands on your head,
feel the softness of your hair,
trace from your ears to your jaw, your chin,
smooth under your eyes with my thumb,
run my finger down your nose, from the bridge to the soft tip,
mapping what I can, and touch you on the lips,
my hands on your shoulders,
gauging height and span,
smell the dry sun in your hair,
rub smooth perfect thumbnails,
hold your hand and take the angled weight of your arm,
hold me close to know the depth of you,
your contours, scale, and ratios,
speak to me, whisper,
tell me what you see,
because I have yet to see you,
and maybe never will,
and maybe you not me.

MY FINEST HOUR

There was one hour in my life
alive awake conscious
when I held back all my criticisms
of everything that had ever happened
and of everything I had ever done
of every person I hadn't liked
and even more of those I did

that hour held a silent space
where critical thoughts shrank
in their own mirrored sight
the past and I no matter nor consequence
everything and everyone borne by their merits
not by origin, symmetry nor familiarity

outwardly I truly listened
and inward I forgave each misstep
each consideration untethered from what had been
a divine shift towards empathy compassion and truth
even to myself.
That rare hour maybe was my finest.

AT THE END OF THE EARTH

The end is nigh, when not if
telescopes and microscopes and satellites are trained
tracking speed and heading
this way, nothing but dead sea between us,

The end draws near, the horizon draws closer
an inconvenient truth
a world on fire, flooded and poisoned
politics religion justice, all have failed us
as we have failed them all
consumption, corruption, pollution, accelerating
tipping points, critical loss, extinction,

So I ran, far away from civilisation
to the last place on earth,
from the east and the west the currents still sweep the debris
  away
virgin sands, crystal waters
blue glass curling and gently breaking
somewhere behind the sun-capped peaks
the world is warring, hastening its demise
hungry extraction, refined concentration, toxic obsolescence
landfill landscapes growing, glowing
while refugees hold out . . .
no dignity in poverty,
no dignity in riches,
no glorious empire,

Let the silk run through your hands
let the water tide-mark the contours of your body
see how the sun lifts everything in view
so beautiful, that sadness rises in balance
we will be overrun
an unstoppable wave pushes hard, barely retreating before
  surging again
irresistible,

How lucky we are to see paradise
how we feel we dreamt it all, just by looking away
wasn't this Eden enough
could we not have stayed, it all
even Eden tells of taking more
of self and pride and greed
the seeds of its destruction.

REFLECTIONS

The whole room reflected in the outside, with me looking in
surroundings superimposed and overlaid, in and out,

I saw a version of me, just shadows and highlights
looking back asking the same question,

The glass a double painting, two silent songs sung over each
   other,
one of the trees and the passing day,
the other of me inside this box, broken by the reflection of the
   open sky,

Another looked from outside, seeing himself in my room,
   unseen by me
and a bird swooped overhead, over his head, and to him over
   mine, and his as well
then a bus, heedlessly, drove straight through me,
but which was the ghost, the man in the world of reflections, or
   the bus reflected there,

Houselights in the trees, a ceiling of sky, and me looking for
   answers,
How did I get there, what happened on the way?

STORY OF TREES

Born of different seeds
Spliced grafted
Planted by chance, by the swirl of the wind
Or the planter's design, growing in proximity
Under the same sun, fed through the same water, filtered up
  through different roots
Scorched and sodden by season
Pollinated and fruitful in maturity,
Now gnarled and scarred in places
Still growing in the pattern of each species
Each with a reach and a depth
Rooted and anchored for shelter and strength,
For shade, wider than their silhouette
The north wind bends one and the east wind shakes another
Pushes us together and pulls us apart
Underground talons grip
And ropes and cords and threads criss-cross tightly, holding
  firm
Under shadows overlapping in ever-changing patterns as the
  sun arcs
And still our stories grow
– the axe still seems a long way off.

THE DESCENT

Loosely sliding
and faster
gravity tips
falling
into darkness

rewind the news
reel me out
but unravelling
the return eclipsed

from charcoal light to ink
all I have is what I believe
drowning in the dark
sobbing echoes
in isolation
held together
with invisible cords

some lift
some release
feet touch
hesitant surface
bones take weight
ahead gloom
no longer pitched
wary stumble
past shadows
twilit cavern
and out into the night sky

the distant moon and a handful of stars
half light the way
rest a while
then ascend
with celestial guides
an imprint of fear remains
faithlessness exposed

a hard path leads up
from the valley of the shadow
easing, in your lightening dawn
knowing I had not been alone.

THE DIFFERENCE BETWEEN
MEN AND WOMEN IN SHOES

Men have
A smart pair, and casual pair,
a work pair, and a pair for the garden,
Plus wellington boots, and hiking boots,
and football boots, and trainers for going for a run,
and tennis trainers, and going down the pub trainers.
A pair for every function.
Equipment and uniform.

Women have
A black pair, a brown pair, a cream pair, a red pair,
A high-heeled pair, a low-heeled pair, and flats,
Crocodile, suede and leather,
Everyday, fancy - for weddings,
and for popping to the shops,
Knee-high, shin high, toeless,
Gappy, strappy, flip-floppy, trotty,
For teetering and tottering,
Slip-slapping and smacking,
A pair for every outfit, climate and mood,
And every combination.

It's always justified,
No one denies.

BLOOD IS RED

Red blood
Dark skin

Light skin
Blue shirt
Badge

beaten Black and Blue
Red dries Black

took a knee in Red and Gold
to Outcry

Blue shirt
knee to neck,
to Ash
Final.
finally, Outcry

children open your eyes
the grown-ups cannot explain
how accidents of birth
determine your worth

history has polarised
the beauty in our spectrum
and weak men do drive a wedge
of hatred born in fear

Blood is Red
tears are Clear
in all God's children
a spectrum, a graduation
not Black and White,
nor Red-skinned, nor Yellow
one race, one Adam
revealed, in many cultures, many traditions

but history is angry with injustice
awake to the heritage of privilege
all slaves to legacy
built on sin
that chokes futures

Blood is Red
and washes pure
save us from our sins

AFTERGLOW

wasps soothing buzz
licking the dregs of empty glasses
tiptoeing across the table
stumbling over crumbs
the summer sun hanging high
heat smells of dry hay
sleepy children with sticky lips lost to their shaded dreaming
hazy afterglow
drinking in the peace

WAITING IN THE DARK

Take the volume from the incessant chatter
snuff the blazing lights
sit down in darkness
comforted by patience

Stretched between twitching hope
and the sleep of nostalgia
the comfort of newness, of possible change
or the embrace of the rush of the familiar

Wandering from one day to the next
with no race to run
no flames to feed
the metronome clocks
another day
that slips spent to the pile

I sit in the dark
fix on one dim shape
and build around that reality
rebuild a sense of me
that has been dismantling

Washing dressing eating working
scrolling, petitioning
wishing for time travel
either forwards or back

Waiting in the rain of speculation
for a cure, a believable all-clear, or a way out
waiting for the same again, again
to stay safe is to stay still, and let go
accept this is out of my hands

Sweet nostalgic music has lost all meaning
return to that country cut off by shifting plates
lose myself in stranger sounds, for stranger times
textural landscapes, shapes and patterns
that emerge from groans and clangs
Sylvian and Sakamoto
T.Rex and Tom Waits
from a different time
a different place
to repaint the here and now

So I sit in night
shrouded in the weight of these times
while shadow dogs guard me
sinking into the comfort of the dark

UP THERE

Up there
On the stair
Is where, I sat
Listening in
Barefoot and pyjama-d
In the comforting sound of adult conversation
Six or eight voices, out of range
All the edges knocked off and muffled

Listening in also
For the tread, closer
And the pull of the door on the carpet
Someone coming to check the oven
A swift and quiet retreat
As the chatter bounced out into the hallway
and up the stairs after me

Voices clear, recognisable,
Overlapping each other
Until the door pushes to again
The dinner checked and stirred
And I creep back down
As far as I dare,
No man's land beneath me
Get caught there, sent back to bed
Tummy-ache or can't sleep fooling no one
And everyone will know

Up there
On the stair
The bridge between sleep and grown-ups
Just sit and stay as long as you can
Until they troop out for their dinner
Younger then than I am now

Older and I'm there
On the stair
Creeping back in
Don't dare wake
Who might clock the time
Miss the step that creaks
Tread the edge
of the one that groans in the middle

Even now I know the routine
Plane tickets printed but still in the tray
Remembered at midnight for early flights
Still got the moves,
in and out

I have my own stairs now
It's not quite so much fun
Up there

MOMENT OF RECOGNITION

The first few notes and you know where they lead
a description that someone else wrote that chimes,
a moment of emotion in song that holds you,
a sense of unsaid understanding found in a poem
a movement in a piece of music that aligns somewhere and
  carries you along

the untangling of thoughts into patterns and shapes,
untangled unconsciously by these forms of art

the truth of science
the mystery of faith
the comfort of love

when the work of someone who's never known you,
lets you feel like they do,
and you want them to talk some more, about you

a face in the crowd, who sees you too.

MOVING BACK IN

The annual blue tits have returned
and the goldfinch
to flit and chatter
and peck out fresh buds,
unperturbed by mankind's crisis.

Then one day a pheasant, a pheasant,
took a walk across our suburban patch
and then more game, a red legged partridge,
said Google,
ventured, from his estate to ours.

They say noise pollution is down
and the wildlife is moving back in
though this high street is noisy with buses and boy-racers,
with footfall at the chemist opposite.

Our robin is quietened –
a pair of magpies scouting out a location, location,
and a pair of cloaked ravens flap fingered wings
their flight path ignoring the parallel lines
that mark our domains.

Foxes who tore open rubbish on Sunday nights
now openly pad across lawns, leaping fences,
no news of poisoned bats to disturb their play.

No facemasks, no lockdown, no travel bans,
nature runs free while we stand still,
watching.

THIN AIR

It's an untethered balloon
already out of reach

It's a pub-quiz answer
you know you know but can't recall

on the tip of your tongue
but no further

It's the reason you are at the top of the stairs, wondering
and the reason you will have to go back down, empty handed

I had an idea
so clear and brilliant
that I didn't write it down . . .

I know it exists by the hole it left behind
I can't picture the picture
behind that negative space

I need a clue (or two)
to re-board that train of thought

It's escaped
like space junk,
floating away . . .

WHO YOU DO NOT RECOGNISE

you see glimpses
shades and angles
of things you might remember, but
you no longer trust them

seeds that grew
into different trees
with stranger fruit

those years away
took your children
and gave you these people
in their place

smiles and touches
a kiss an embrace
exaggerate the lives
you do not recognise

you try to connect
but each enquiry is diverted
in the mirror you search
but they don't appear

a tree grows in scale
while a butterfly is
a magician's trick
inside a cocoon –
what caused you to spin it
what happened inside?

my children have disappeared
the change severe
I do not think they are
who they say they are

FLOATING FREE

the tide pushes me further from the shore
towards the deep end of the ocean
my feet leave the bottom
reaching not finding
certainty swept away
grounding gone I float free
no anchors, the tide can decide

waves which have travelled from beyond the horizon
raise me onto their shoulders and lower me to their belly
a peak and a valley with each swell

the weight of the ocean could drown me
but I am filled with a relative density, to stay
above the weight of the ocean
to swim with or against the current
and the one who sends the waves
from beyond the horizon

BEFORE

I dreamt of you last night
my friend
We talked for hours
Never getting to why we stopped
We were our best versions
As we always were

The gulf of time and distance
Faded you out
A guess of then not now
Ignoring the years,
Still regretting that last request
When your life resolved
You know I know I was forgiven
Forces of circumstance held me elsewhere

Since then life building far apart
Thinly stretched
So many missing details in the space between us.

*

I spoke to you today
To find the thread a rope, pulling
The gap closing quickly with each word
Decades concertina the past to now
Wildfire recognition

Same you, in darker troubles,
Only asking for songs
sent by the dozen
Still both knowing
We are old memories
Who last forever

MACHINERY OF PRODUCTION

All hands to the pump
All flying beasts to the fields, the trees, the hedgerows
The invitation of spring
To match-make furiously
And weave a pattern of fertility

Here comes the summer of the good hard work
The labours of production

Capture the urging sun in cells
Roots reach reach
Draw nutrients and drink
Every plant filling to burst

Stalks shoot up like adolescents
Fields sway like a thousand dancers
The wheat tans gently
Fruit sweetens and blushes ripe
Heat and sun, sun and heat
Interspersed with welcome rain

Spring flowers overtaken
By rosettes and buttonholes
Peony, rose and hollyhocks
Summer's wedding flowers

A spirit of growth and grace
A blessing of the fruits upon the people
The harvest will be abundant
Joy of collaboration, cooperation
Hearty effort all

These slowly shortening days of light
Of heat and growth and swelling
A festival of red gold green love
Nature fulfilling its ancient calling

ANARCHY IN A SMALL TOWN

Some seized the bank, until the cash was spent
Some seized the bakery, until the flour ran out
Some seized the pub, a short-term solution
The suppliers would not restock,

Some appropriated the library
In quiet, without a single crossed word
In broad daylight, uncontested,

And they read the books
And spoke out the poems
And acted out the plays to each other
Until all's imagination was fit to burst, freshly every day,

The doors were left open,
To let in the poor, the hungry and the hungover,
And we read together of economics and cuisine
and medicine by day,
Replenishing their losses,
And fables and ghost stories and prayers by night,
Adding to our wealth,

The only rules were don't misfile the book that feeds you
nor crease nor tear,
and always use a bookmark,
For while books are just paper and words are just letters,
and letters just shapes on a page,
Facts are facts, opinions are opinions
and flights of fantasy are real indeed to those in the reading.

When we are brave we will go back out and work out our place
  in the world
and always come back to this
our school, our playground, our sanctuary

UNHEARD

The train passes regularly, noisily, greedily
The widow's concerns unaddressed

The hands judder round, silently now
No hour by hour alerts, or second by second reminders
As time will run out

The blanket sky hides the progress of the sun
Rivers deepen, glaciers evaporate, tinder scorched
Changes unremarked, 'til compressed condensed concentrated
Natural evolution animated to trigger
Accelerators released

Bones calcify, follicles fade,
Senses strain, the fountain runs dry
The widow sleeps at peace
Windows closed to the passing trains
The clock still counting down

TEN THINGS FOUND IN A TIME

TRAVELLER'S BACKPACK

1. One Polaroid of Henry VIII being kissed passionately, by a lady not wearing a crown
2. Football scores torn from newspapers dated May 1981
3. A wanted poster of himself in a cowboy hat
4. A life insurance policy renewal reminder letter
5. A dvd box marked Top Secret containing a disc of *Back To The Future*
6. A Post-It that says 'Remember to drop off at publishers ! ! ' – stuck to
7. A small note book, handwritten in code, except 'JFK, the truth, OMG', on the first page
8. An ornate key wrapped in a red ribbon, a hint of perfume
9. A black box, one red light blinking, labelled Property of Intergalactic Space Force
10. A receipt from the Titanic Lounge Bar – whisky no ice

NEW NAME

If I wanted to give myself a new name
a name with no prior connotations
no acquaintances, nor celebrities, nor notable namesakes
whether awful or saintly, couldn't be considered,
If I wanted to give myself a new name I would,
but every name is known, somewhere.

I chose instead to make up a new name,
untainted by association,
but even those attempts had connotations
of origin, of gender, of decisions of pronunciation.

I tried long combinations of syllables,
and single syllables,
but every sound has been made before.
I tried reducing to just the letters of the alphabet,
but Gee sounded American, Elle was French, Aye was Scottish,
and being called Why would need explaining.

So I'm back where I started,
with the name my parents gave me,
before they knew who I was,
only an idea, an association, of who they hoped I would be.

Seems it's up to me
to give this name
something to live up to.

VALENTINE

The least romantic day of the year has passed on
Today no guilty flowers, dutiful cards, unwanted chocolates
Spontaneity will be back on the menu
Expressions of love that sing solo,

That shabby prince steps back into the cog of days
Shamelessly counting his takings
ignoring the cynicism and unwanted attention,

Yes, spontaneity is back on the streets
Scratching, purring, roaring
Bumbling, stumbling, gushing
Declaring, swearing, promising
Risking it all again,

SHARP

so sharp not felt
painless entry fools me again
medication forced
a ball-bearing brooding under skin
so slowly seeping into me

vein valve stretched
a pool accumulates
pulling veins and valves further
blood slowed to thick
pressure building 'til

pain, like reminders after years of drunk
hijacks, cripples
the thought of it receding
just enough to bear

watch the tip enter silently again
efficiently sharp
navel clockface, hours marked
before pills and tests and decisions

TAKE A MOMENT

Just take a moment to breathe
as Jesus took his first breathe
And take another
as he gave up his last
the whole of God's love, holiness and mercy
lived out between those two breaths

Take a moment to see
see how he came
The humblest of origins
No privilege for this Prince, of Peace,
the Word of God made flesh

Relinquishing the glory of heaven
and the intimacy of the Father
dependent on the Holy Spirit
Born to a disgraced young woman
and her humbled husband
Lain in a feeding trough
to be honoured by night workers

Take a moment to wonder
where were the other relatives of Joseph
called to the census in Bethlehem
Could they not find room in their lodgings,
in their hearts for Mary,
No bed, no dignity, no compassion
Take a moment to see
who today has no bed, no dignity
is afforded no compassion?
Don't let Christmas obscure the truth

And wise and educated men came
but not from the palace or the priesthood
But foreigners from the East
with their symbolic gifts
Led by a star,
followed with faith and understanding
Let us be led by signs and wonders too
followed by faith and understanding

And take a moment to see
the family's flight to Egypt
Refugees with a child, stateless and status-less
Running from persecution
to the land of the Pharaohs
who had enslaved their ancestors
As we were once enslaved, by sin
by greed, and pride

See patient Mary, waiting,
Thirty years of knowing who he was
pondering how this could be
Let us ponder how this could be
knowing we all should die, all except he
that's how he saves us, undeserved
the only one who needn't die

Take a moment to see
the violence that followed his birth
for threatening power and prestige
would return and put him to death
for threatening power and prestige
Such are human hearts
blind to his selfless love

to his healing and miracles and acceptance
mankind's contempt for the life that has been granted
and He who gives us life

And the life of Jesus,
between those two breaths
was a gift of love, that brings us life
The star shining in the darkness
proclaiming everlasting life

Just take a moment to consider
so many people in the world this Christmas
They all need what you have
– hope in Jesus

EYES SOFTLY SHUT

With your eyes softly shut
Like a baby
I watch you sleep

How long since someone watched over you?
She would have, while she could

As you trust your being to safety in sleep
Do you dance in the other
Or sing with the angels?

Do you sleep so lightly because they left you so young?
Not safe to dream with careless abandon
You sleep so lightly my gaze will wake you
As you stir somewhere inside
And open your eyes
I close mine, before you know

As you wake your years give you weight
And substance to the dreams you'll remember
Mine senseless fragments growing fainter
Yours so clearly defined

BLACKOUT

This is how it is
No matter how I wish

Resist the closing circle
And break your heart to care
Tears congregate
Stinging for the lost
Already hollowed out

Life's poetry stifled
While nothing matters
Indulgence sickens
Distractions ignored
Trapped in fear

The air will be a vacuum
And my lungs will burn

Meet me brother at the corner
Don't let them see your face
Greet me with your voice
Standing back to back
And tell me how it is

A circle of self
values simplified
responds to any kind face

the future stripped
the present undoes
stay still
only reach slowly

waves crash outside
invading my head
ripples splintered

a lifetime of
meaningless milestones
pointless collecting, curating
significance reversed
masks dissolve
nothing to hide

blasting high, delays
only reality

art is us
self expression
the final refuge
the freedom illusion betrayed
nucleus recentres quickly
promised recoveries poisoned
by false nostalgia

come sit with me
in Eden's ruins
I cannot repay
With what you need

Thoughts slip unfinished
Lost or locked to themselves,
Inseparable and incomplete

Tomorrow will come
for some

BOY SOLDIER

A life ambushed before it's ever begun
an orphan soldier at the end of a gun
it takes a village to raise a child
but that village
is razed to the ground,

Violence, no child should witness
allegiance demanded buries revenge
burning, fear hate hardens,
and infects the next,

Out of darkness
a knife slashes
rifle ready he shoots
his mother's scared face falls away
wakes in cold sweat again,

Proven promoted rewarded
a circle of abuse perpetuates
the shiver on his heart
his life a shadow,

Everything he was meant to be
grows ever fainter,
memories beaten bloody silenced
calling from a prison truck
just faces of the dead,

His future locked
on a path that narrows
to an end
his story will not be told
just another corpse to clear away.

WAKE

I want to wake within this life
Not dozing through another siren
To see quite clearly what is there
No hazy intervals of uncertainty
To hear to smell to touch the actual design
Not filtered through a mind on pins
Touching only on the sharp
While all the more is guessed or believed
From others in their own

But if I woke to all these truths
My heart could not fit them in
Nor my eyes, my mind, could comprehend
So stretched that I would fall apart
And lose the sense of everything

But if my heart could grow with time
And my waking be in the same stride
My eyes would see it all as wide
And slowly filling expands my mind

Then in the end maybe I would
Be wakeful to it all

THE CARPENTER

The carpenter hammered to a tree
The counsellor abandoned
The merciful punished
The blameless mocked
The healer damaged
The gardener wrapped in thorns
The light of the world entombed

And then

More than a victory,
an overturning, an undoing
Untouchable
No longer a matter of judgement, but an invitation
Asking, will you follow?

BUNK BEDS, HIGHFIELD ROAD

Tucked up in bed
She read us stories
of talking elephants
of Max and the Wild Things
of loaves and fishes,
One up one down
pyjamas and brushed teeth
prayers with eyes closed
and his sandpaper cheek goodnight

My aunty came to sit with me
after he fell out of the bunk bed,
They all went to the hospital
to have his head checked,
Breakfast was different that day

I don't remember the heatwave
I do remember the cracking storm that broke
outside the window

JIGSAW

Impressionist fragments
Colours fade and bleed indistinct
Trying each piece with each piece
Seems tedious and forever

But eyes recalibrate, microscope
Scanning each free piece
Identifying dots edges shapes and gradients
Cross checked against the master

A spot finds the exact place
Or precise angle and shadow align
Every detail pin sharp to the eye
Connections fit and fill the frame

A life of fragments
Slowly building progress except
Some pieces float unconnected still
No master for reference

At the end all will be arranged
The picture fully emerged and
every continuation understood

I cannot see the distant detail
nor even the walls of the room
But the blurred are clear
the vague distinct
the minute easy to read
until this picture is complete

STRANGE WHAT YOU REMEMBER

I don't remember the food at all
but I do remember the meal
I do remember the light in your eyes
and your hair shadowed, framing your face

I remember opportunities for being funny
being polite, and knowledgeable and interested
and not being shy of any.
I do remember what you said, I can replay it all

I'm trying not to read too much, just enjoying the memory
not convicting myself of mistakes, or accusing myself of
   misinterpretation

I remember the journey home
reliving every highlight
regretting only that it hadn't lasted longer

Hoping above all that the best version of me
had won you over,
even if you didn't yet know

I do remember the food, just not the taste
only the consumption and the wine
and the light in your eyes, I might have mentioned

I remember acting like a grown-up, really
with confidence, generous, drawing you out
and finding a new me, restored
one that I liked, one I liked being
one that I think you found in me
one that might last
until we meet again

I remember that there were other people there
but not exactly why
I don't remember anything I said
except everything I said to you

I remember clearly saying goodbye
prior arrangements followed through
I remember you turned to wave us off
hoping that was a message for me

PARROTS AT IGUASSU

Gold jacketed
Red sashed
Aqua shirted
And emerald breaches
Screeching their possessive strut
Pirates in the trees, bobbing and weaving

We scuttled through, those gangsters mocking
Didn't dally through their patch
Left them kings of their confinement

Cake and rice pudding for breakfast
Mangos in the trees
Barbeque rice black-beans garlic
No one dreams of leaving
Waving at the cosmonauts
Through the cloudless sky

FENCES

The last time we met
on opposite sides of the fence
he asked why I was there.
I believed it was the side to be on.
He told me what I was risking
nothing I didn't already know
stated the danger to my family, my future
nothing we hadn't already overcome
how I didn't owe anyone anything
that I had to look after what was mine.
That's not how I want to live
I chose to be here, on this side of the fence

Of course I'd rather be there
on that side of the fence,
protected, comfortable, immune.
More than this I want the fence taken down
these are people not cattle, nor criminal
while the fence is staying up
I'll help as many through, before I claim my right to passage.

He said I was risking nothing and proving nothing
but it seemed to be bothering him enough
to mock me and call me a part-time martyr
I hope somewhere inside he was embarrassed
at wanting to be free to join me, if only for a moment.
You could die here, they could clear the place, and deny you.
Die here or die there, what's the difference

Safety is a luxury
but dreams are essential, essential as blood and air.
This freedom to choose is a privilege
too valuable to ignore, too precious to hide away
Comfort complacency suspicion, these are criminal
He reminded me Charity begins at home.
This is my home, I intend to be charitable

NEW YEAR EVOLUTION

Another pirouette in front of the sun
The first of many 'til we're here again
Unchanged, just nearer the end
Unless, we decide,
Our one true distinction
To alter the path of destiny
Just a nudge, of deliberate intention
New Year evolutions

Burdens ease through repetition
Resolutions broken a hundred times
are kept two hundred and more
Evolution transformation

A resolution shared will nag
A turning wheel keeps turning
against the will to stop

A new leaf turned, and a new leaf turned
By the end of a year, a volume,
An album of friends, a room full of memories
Changes that have stayed
Steps add up, the penny jar fills

You may not have reached the top of the mountain
But you've still improved the view

HOLDING ON TO NOTHING

I've been holding onto nothing
wasted all these days
believing all your promises
that you never made

I've been holding onto nothing
ignoring all the signs
it won't be you and me forever
that picture lost in time

I could have started over
I could have seen the truth
I wish someone had told me
but I did deny the proof

I've been holding onto nothing
in a story I wrote alone
caught up in the moment
when I really should have known

I didn't realise that you'd left
cos you were still around
but miles away in your heart
you weren't waiting to be found

Why did I hand it over?
so sure, so readily
when a hard-fought thing has more worth
and your heart was not for me

I lost you in the dark
not realising that you'd gone
I thought you were beside me
listening to the storm

I've been singing to the silent stars
telling you how I felt
you're too busy rearranging
the hand that you've been dealt

I've been holding onto nothing
writing songs you'll never hear
'cos you left some time ago
it's just becoming clear

I've been holding onto nothing
that I wanted to believe
and this is not the first time
there's a pattern now I see

THE GLORIOUS RESTRUCTURE

We set sail unaware, and then
one third must go they said
It's all we can afford
and those who remain will be empowered
to work another half again
we'll work smarter not harder they said
but smarter sounded like harder after all

We'll pay you to jump now,
or less to jump later
and then we won't pay you to jump at all,
just sink, or swim

empire building with heads in the clouds
has emptied out the funds
it seems we are not carrying gold
but only bricks and mortar

each third oar was empty
pull harder was the cry
and life jackets must be worn
if they don't square the books
we'll all be walking the plank

now I am rearranged
three in place of five
hearts and souls withdrawn, reserved,
held in cheque
resilience thin where loyalty lay

we've reduced the weight, made it easier for you,
so row faster, otherwise we'll all sink
we didn't need them, just filling seats,
and pulling oars we didn't need

never mind what's always been said
'It's the staff that make this place'
never mind just to see where the pieces fall,
and some will fall to pieces

we'll work smarter not harder they said
but smarter was harder after all.

MAYAKOVSKY SWAGGER

We're cutting the workforce by three in ten
The devil whistles this is the end, just for you

It's all we can afford
and those who remain will be empowered
to work another half again

We know you are concerned
but we will do everything we can
except guarantee your concerns
they didn't say in so many words

You'll pour the marbles on the board
see which holes are filled,
and some will roll off,
and no openings remain

At the clearest point when all was empty
and I needed to reinvent
a kindly soul asked after me.
asked of future plans,
I had no answer at that point
Considering my options
I hinted at an angry poem,
all my woes laid bare,
he wished me luck and said to give it
"a bit of Mayakovsky swagger"

Intrigued inspired I sought him out,
quite mad,

swaggering, staggering
swatting and on the verge of sarcastic collapse,
Mayakovsky that is,
not my learned friend

I imagine he'd say "unsheathe your sword,
 and give them both barrels
slash an opening though the veil,
and stand upon a ledge
with one hip forward, one arm outstretched, pointing to the
  future,
on, come on to the promised land"

I was petering out, a landslide in shoes,
not listed in our glorious future
What would this Vladimir have said?

Meanwhile lies circulate
of Europe's intentions, of immigration,
of the state of the planet,
of what our leaders believe in,
and how much you can trust science,

empires built by slaves
on shoulders falling one by one
now the faith has gone
pacing on this shrinking iceberg
be gone, poor romantic soul

Not rising as a phoenix,
but as a man half-drowned,
weak from exertion
and coughing up bile.

between troughs of despondency and soul weariness,
I heard again, "give it some Mayakovsky swagger"

For Mayakovsky rallied with the duke
"as you limp across the summer
festering wounds and gaping holes
imagine a sword on your belt
rest your hand on its hilt
look 'em in the eye and say
you, you are only a cloud in trousers,
one swirl one split
one sunny day and you are gone
one split in your breeches is all it takes

which faceless fools overloaded the boat
and cried row faster we're sinking
unmask them"

But the captain held the keys to the brig,
and the key to the rum ration too
and the wages ledger was in his grasp
and we were powerless to act.

The officers they scuttled out the back door
to lifeboats with oars and sails
their golden goodbyes muffled

arbitrary brutality,
oil-spill disdain,
everything black and unclean-able

Angry at the waste, the stress,
the toxic levels of anxiety that change our chemical composi-
  tions,

seep battery fluids into our muscles
and poison neural networks.

I fear young Mayakowsky would have felt this longer than I
And fallen into drunk delirium,
Or crude torment and despair

Now they say the finances have righted,
there's some money to be spent
I don't know whether to laugh or cry
or burn the place to the ground
"give it some Mayakovsky swagger"

No it wasn't a great summer,
the stress echoes on after the pressure is released,
deep stretch marks represent,
the relief turns to anger for the journey to that point.

The pendulum kept swinging
Mayakovsky whispered
"Band together and fight,
be anarchists for a day, and a night,
and see without regret what remains in the morning."

UNWINDING HISTORY

(or if I could turn back Cher)

If you could unwind history how far back would you go?
Are we not doomed to repeat?
even taking with you what you now know,

There must be an alternative forward
from a time before the pandemic?
How far back gives us time to swerve it,
and who would even listen?
What might we lose in the new route forward?

If you went back before Hitler,
his Holocaust, his Solution
how far back would you have to go?
Back before Hitler and before the conditions which brought
  him to power,
and the events that led to those conditions,
and the situation whose consequences were those events,
and then before whatever led to all that.

You can try to hold the spring to stop a clock ticking
but as soon as you let go time is in motion again.

Can you stop Mao, Pol Pot, and Stalin?
Go back to before slavery – but how to prevent it?
happening as it did.

Back to before the moment when these events occurred
to when the plan was made,

when the idea found favour,
to when the conditions of nature and future and time and place
  coincided
and before the path was set.

As you erase each problem you keep retreating into the past
and erasing the future we know.

And what might we lose or delay –
a man on the moon, the internet,
microwave ovens, or sliced bread, the best thing?

Keep going and you'll be erasing the Romans and their cruelty,
Will that erase Christ?
But if those prophecies were always true, and he was destined?
and if you go back to before those prophecies,
back to Adam
mankind will still make it happen,
the snake, the fruit, Cain killing Abel, and on,

It seems human history cannot be truly untangled
because it is a pattern doomed to repeat.

No storms no peace,
no struggle no relief,
no work, no prize.

So, no Cher, if you could turn back time it wouldn't do much
  good,
the clock would resume ticking.
Eventually all those things you now regret
you would still have said
because that's who you are and how you feel.
If you could turn back time you wouldn't know

how far back to go, to find a new path
where it wouldn't happen all over again with the same guy.

Is this poem fatalistic or merely logical?
Is it even a poem?

Or we need to find the perfect parallel universe,
and parachute ourselves in?
without disturbing anything
And would such a place be empty of the free-willed fully human.

How can you stop the tide of evil that ebbs and flows in man-
  kind's heart?
surging forward with aggression and greed,
and pulling back in fear and suspicion

However far you could turn back time
would not man's spilt blood still creep forward,
staining every history?

GHOSTS

Our ghosts play on
While we wash and change
And weary back to work

The empty hall echoes in our absence
As he flicks the ball up so he can turn and volley
As another runs hard, chops back and shoots
As he slides past obstacles and hammers one goalward
While urgent messages bounce off the walls, coded,
A pass goes astray, is not forthcoming, too early too late,
Or follows a perfect trajectory, picks out, pinpoint
As he fills the space obscuring the target, no sense no feeling –
  no goal

All the shirts don't match, training tops, replicas, vintage
and the teams reshuffle each week

A player slaloms smoothly, the ball always in possession, rolling.
Another stands over the ball, teases, twitches, waiting for the
  moment
One runs onto the ball, ignores shouts to shoot and plays in
  another,
Another holds the ball ignoring pleas to pass,
keeps the ball out of reach until, left foot, bam !
Another lets off a volley, of how unhappy he is with his team
These boys are chameleons, serious then smiles, real wild cards

Others came and went,
retired, moved on, but you,
You were taken from us,

And every reminder puts you back in the hall
in triumph or dismay, treating each with good humour

A cry for a foul, handball, disputed goal, disputed score,
a pass, an apology, proper marking,
all echo around while we wait for the next match.

Your ghost is in there too, finding space, trapping neatly,
holding up and driving one through.

The ghosts play on, organised or shambolic,
winning by teamwork, or individual skills and passion,
lucky bounce, unlucky deflection, patient decision or rash folly,
zig zag passes finished crisply,
unstoppable, blocked, intercepted, breakaway,
no one's tracking back!

Appreciation grown over time,
of who and what we are,
respect friendship analysis

Blood sweat and tears, mostly sweat

Our ghosts they play on,
long after the inquest for this week's game has ended,
waiting for our return.

ARC OF THE DIVERS

Still
reach
bounce
launch
twist
unwind
to tuck
spin
unfold
spear
disappear
splish

Clean lines, so clean it wipes the memory,
the sensation is all that remains

They know
how they executed
For us, the slow motion replay;

Parallel synchronicity,
Where every flaw would be exposed,
a graceful flawless elegance.
Twisting like tree ornaments in the wind
Spinning like clockwork, the inner wheels
Every frame a picture of grace and tension
Out of the tuck to break the plane together
Leaving two puffs of water
As if they had shot into another dimension

They'll show that replay again.

MEMORIES AND SECRETS

Back then we all had secrets,
private and treasured
when we were young and new
with impetuous hearts
wide-eyed at life, drinking in hard

secrets of cliff edges that held our breathe,
hidden beauty we thought only we could see,
of secret places to swim in deep blue waters,
and to fly to at night, while others slept

secrets of fires, and fears and foolishness
some shared, confessed with strict boundaries,
loosened out at the end of exhausting days,

all those secret places are in another country now
does the recollection of summer bring a glow to your skin?
do you have enough memories to keep you warm through the
   winter?
now we are older and those secrets are lifeless, even the raging
   fires

without memories what is a man?
without knowledge of his own history
his anchors, his secret places
his pivotal moments and formative years
the crutches when his heart was broken, deceived,
or lifted in victory and triumph

without memories what is a man?
is he free, or merely a shell?
Unbound, or lost forever?

SHORT STORIES / PROSE

OUT OF ORDER

Today is Tuesday. I have to be very careful with everything I do, because yesterday was Wednesday and if I can't join today neatly with yesterday there will be gaps for chaos to slip through.

Yesterday was tomorrow (Wednesday) but the day before was Monday. I was straddling the gap all day yesterday, trying to guess what would happen in between, wishing I'd paid attention on Monday to what was going on and where it might lead. Tomorrow maybe we'll be back in order.

Tomorrow had better be Thursday because whatever chaos gets through tonight I'll be spending all day straightening it out. I can't be thinking about, if it's Friday when does Thursday come in, or if it's a week on Saturday whether I should note down the football scores and place a bet ready for whenever this Saturday decides to show up.

Up to this Monday I'd only ever had the slightest sense of déjà vu, zoning out with the ironing, thoughts wandering, time fluid, but never this. Maybe tomorrow will be Christmas and I'll know what to buy the kids, instead of just hoping for the best. Maybe it'll all work itself out, the only chaos will be the usual, non-time/space continuum chaos. Otherwise by Christmas there'll be so much built up I might as well declare the apocalypse.

Yesterday Dad asked me how today Tuesday had been, which hadn't happened yet. What could I say?

Maybe I should go and see him, but if yesterday, which was tomorrow, he hadn't seen me the day before (that is today), will that create two of him? one that saw me on Tuesday and one that didn't, or will that cancel him out, cancelling me out, unravelling history back to the point of his first influence? Chaos everywhere.

I had an email today reminding me to pay the gas bill, so do I pay it today? I didn't pay it yesterday (which is tomorrow) so is it okay to pay today which is yesterday's yesterday. I think I'll leave it.

And there was a cake in the tin yesterday that's not there now, it looked home-made and untouched – did I make it? did someone bring it round? did I buy it from a door-to-door cake salesman?

It's Schrodinger's cake – it's only there today if tomorrow you opened the tin.

If it's not there by the end of the today then it won't be there tomorrow which was yesterday, when I saw it. So . . .

If I don't get this right there could be a black hole at the bottom of the cake tin, and I'd hate to cause the end of time and space over a misplaced Victoria sandwich.

PLEASE LET IT BE SO

A few years from now –
- *Daddy, what did you do in the climate protests?*
- I met your mum. And we sang songs. And we sat in the road,
- *You sat in the road? Isn't that dirty?*
- It was, but if we sat in the road then the lorries couldn't drive to where they were going?
- *Didn't that make the lorry drivers angry?*
- Yes some of them, some said they'd run us over, and some of them said "well done mate, I've got kid's too, (but next time give us some warning)".
- *So did you just sit there?*
- We did.
- *And what happened?*
- The police came along and asked us to move but we stayed there, so they arrested us.
- *Shouldn't you do what a policemen tells you?*
- Yes, but … it's not always … sometimes you have to … you have to think about it the day before, that you might want to get arrested and go to jail.
- *Did you go to jail?*
- Yes,
- *And mummy?*
- Yes, she was sitting next to me, holding hands with me on one side and your uncle Andy on the other. Other times we were chained together with padlocks the police couldn't unlock, but that time, the first time, the plan was to make it easy.
- *So it was okay because you were with mummy?*
- Yes, and we knew we had to get everyone to notice what we were doing so they would talk about it. We wanted to get on the news, not to be famous, but so lots of other people would

see and want things to change too. You remember when you got your bike but you didn't want to ride it because you thought you'd fall off? And then your friend Amy came round and showed you she could do it, and then you gave it a try. It was just like that, if people could see we could do it, they could do it too.

- *So that's why you were sitting in the road?*
- Yes, because we needed lots of people to join in the climate protest. We needed lots of people to do it so we couldn't be ignored,
- *Why do you need lots of people?*
- If I sat in the road right now, on my own, you'd wouldn't join me. You'd think silly daddy, making his trousers dirty.
- *I'd stand on the pavement and shout "quick mummy's coming".*
- You would, you'd think "Daddy must be careful not to be run over". But because there were lots of us, and we had flags and drums and songs they couldn't ignore us and they couldn't run us all over.
- *So it was fun?*
- It was fun but it was important too. We had to do it carefully and together. And it was worth it, because we stopped it didn't we. Because we started something they had to take notice of.
- *So what happened after the police arrested you and mummy?*
- We were put in a police van, with lots of other people who had been sitting down in the road, and we went to jail. We all had our own room, and we just waited, and at midnight they let us go.
- *Why's that?*
- I think the policemen wanted to join in with us more than they wanted to arrest us – plus the paperwork.
- *So you weren't you angry with the police?*
- No they were only doing their job, which is just what we wanted.

Two hours later –
- *So Daddy, you know when you were sitting in the road with mummy, holding hands –*
- Yes?
- *And you wanted everyone to notice –*
- Yes,
- *Did they notice you? – were you on television?*
- We were on the news programme, lots of times. And as more people joined in, it was on the news more and more. All the protests everywhere, all around the world. In some countries the police weren't very nice but the people didn't give up. When you're a bit older they'll teach you about it at school, how all the carbon in the air was making the world hotter, and how dangerous that was.
- *Were you really on the television?*
- Yes, and mummy was interviewed one time about what we were doing.
- *Mummy? Did she look pretty on the television?*
- Yes, and clever, pretty and clever because she had all the answers, she knew about carbon footprints and sustainable energy, and environmental vandalism and plastic pollution. And how the poorest people of the world would be affected worst. Whatever they asked her she could tell them what was wrong and how to change it,
- *Were you asked questions by the man on the television Daddy?*
- No.
- *Oh, why not?*
- Oh I think they liked mummy better because she was so pretty and clever. If you want to get everyone's attention then you can make a lot of noise like we did sitting in the road, or you can speak clever sensible things that everyone can under-stand and agree with, and mummy is very good at that,
- *And everyone agreed with mummy?*

- Nearly everyone, in the end. Other times there were famous people talking about it, actors and politicians and footballers and singers and eventually nearly everyone was talking about it and asking the important people in the government and the business to change things. And the children in school were talking about it.
- *We get told off for talking toooo much.*
- Well this was much naughtier than talking in class. Some of the young people said "this is important we want to join in". But they had to go to school, and they weren't allowed to get arrested. But they weren't happy that the important people who make the rules weren't doing anything about the problem of climate change.
- *So what happened?*
- The children went to school but sometimes on a Friday they would say we're not going to school because there's no point going to school if the planet is dying.
- *It was dying?*
- It was sick and no one could make it better on their own. We all had to make it better together. So the children said we're not going to school on Fridays. Not to be naughty but to show everyone how important it was to them too.
- *Did they get in trouble?*
- Some did, and some didn't because their mums and dads already knew it was important and agreed with what they were doing. And some didn't go to school because they really were naughty and didn't want to go to school anyway, before they understood about the planet dying.
- *So can I not go to school some days?*
- If you have a very good reason, a very very good reason, like it's the day to save the world again, then it's okay. But if you do go to school you'll learn how to keep us safe and keep the world out of trouble for ever.
- *So if I need to save the world I can miss school.*

- Yes, of course, but do ask mummy first.

Next day –
- *Daddy?*
- Yes?
- *Yesterday you said you were sitting in the road to get the important people to listen.*
- Yes, we wanted so many of us to get put in jail that they'd wonder what was going on.
- *What was jail like?*
- Oh don't worry, this was the small jail at the police station, not the big jail where they send the criminals.
- *And the police locked up everyone who was in the van with you?*
- It wasn't just us, there were lots more vans full of people like us, and on the news they said there were too many and the police had to stop arresting people because the police stations were full, at least a thousand people.
- *A thousand people, all in jail!*
- Just to make the important people in the government and running the businesses see it was serious, and important. More important than them, which took a long time. The trees that clean the air were being chopped down, and where the polar bears live the ice was melting which made the sea bigger. You remember when we made sandcastles and when the tide came in it was all knocked over. When the sea got too big that happened to real houses, and people died and some poor people lost everything.
- *All because the important people wouldn't listen to you and mummy?*
- And all the scientists and the activists. Food wasn't growing properly because it was too hot, and all the insects were dying,
- *Insects like flies? – you don't like flies.*
- Not just flies but the bees as well, and we need bees.
- *To make honey, mmmm honey.*

- Not just honey, see the plants that make food have flowers and the special bits of the flowers called pollen have to be mixed up so the plants can start to make the food, like apples and potatoes and tomatoes. And because the bees are so small and clever they go buzzing from one flower to another to another mixing up the pollen from one flower with the next one. But if the bees don't do it the plants don't make the food,
- *Bees go buzzing and have furry bottoms.*
- They do, but they were dying out.
- *Why?*
- You see, the insects eat some of the food or spoil them, and lots of the farmers didn't want the insects around so they sprayed the plants with a poison that kills the insects, but then there weren't enough bees to mix up the pollen, and the poison was making humans ill too.
- *So they stopped?*
- Eventually, and now the numbers of bees and the other insects that mix the pollen are getting better, and the food is better because some of the poison was getting in the food, and now it's not allowed.
- *Good, because I don't want to eat poison,*
- Nobody does, but it took a long time to change the way the businesses grew their food. That was just one of the things that had to change.
- *And it changed because you and mummy sat in the road?*
- Not just us, thousands of us, in the end. Because there were so many things that had to change. There were so many problems. Remember after Christmas we asked you to tidy your room because you had all your new things and the wrapping paper we saved and your toys out from when Emilia was here, really messy. And you thought it was too much to do and you cried, and you didn't want to because you wanted to play instead.
- *There was so much mezziness to tidy up.*

- And we helped you, and we tidied up somethings and then we went and played for a bit and came back and did some more, and together we did tidy everything up together.
- *I never thought we could do it but we did it.*
- We did, and the planet was like that, too much to do, carbon in the air, and plastic in the sea, and people making things and then throwing them away and making more things the same and throwing them away, making a mess, silly really. Like when you made clothes with mummy for Molly, and you dressed her, and then when you made more, and more, we said you had too many and asked you to give some to your cousin, but you hid them under the bed.
- *That was a good hiding place.*
- Yes but what if you had kept making things you didn't need and didn't share. Emilia wouldn't have any clothes for her baby and soon there would be no room under your bed, and your bed would lift of the floor and it would be touching the ceiling and you'd need a ladder to go to bed!
- *So people were hiding things under their beds?*
- No but they were throwing them away, for someone else to find somewhere to put them, and they were still making more, and more. And you know when you make baby clothes there are always bits you've cut off left over, but we can't use them because they are too small.
- *Mummy said they were too small to even make elf's knickers!*
- Rude
- *Rude!*
- So all the left over bits were making a mess too and it was all a waste because people didn't need to make so many new things because they already had too many clothes and phones and cars and shops and plastic bags. But they kept making more.
- *Why? That's silly.*

- Because people were greedy. You remember how you felt when you wouldn't give Emilia those things, remember you said later you didn't like how it felt – greedy and selfish – like you were scared we were going to take them all away, that's how the people with all the things they didn't want to share felt. And there are poorer people all over the world who do need us to share, and to pay them properly for the work they do for us, like sewing together our clothes or putting the inside of our phones together. There's enough for everyone if we share.
- *We're sharing now aren't we?*
- We're sharing more, and helping each other with turning the waste into useful things. And the people who can't grow food are being given enough food and other help. That's what everyone has agreed. The people in charge now know that everyone wants to stop the climate change, and they have to do the things that will make it happen. And so far it looks like we've stopped making the planet more dirty and even hotter, and we've stopped fighting about it for now.
- *That's good isn't it?*
- It is.
- *And there'll be no more fighting . . .*
- We hope so . . . we hope there'll be no more fighting.

LAST CHANCE SALOON

The bell trilled.

Strained conversations withered gratefully.

'Okay everyone, mark your cards and get ready for your final encounter. If you haven't found love at first sight already then don't despair, this could be the one.'

Jake rose from his chair, wiped his still sweaty palms on the back of his jeans, and headed to the final table.

'Nice to meet you,' she called after him.

He turned back, remembering his manners, 'Oh yes, thanks, you too,' and gave a kind but not-interested smile. He'd spent ten minutes nodding politely at her self-absorption, and the flat autumn light hadn't done her face any favours either.

'Before we start on our final round, thank you again for your understanding and like I said you'll all be refunded for this evening, just enjoy yourselves, our gift to you.'

Due to multiple cancellations ('there must be a bug going around') the organisers of today's events had combined the two age groups to have any chance of filling the afternoon. There'd been a few jokes about toyboys and cougars but every-one had voted to carry on.

'Good evening,' said Jake's last chance at a match.

'Good evening to you madam.'

'Janice Smith,' she said, holding out a hand.

'Jake Smith,' he replied taking the hand gently and bowing slightly, 'Coincidence?'

'Maybe we're related?'

'Maybe.'

The following pause was awkwardly long. But what to say?

'So . . .'

'You seem rather young, inexperienced, for this?' said Janice.

'And you seem rather . . . charming, for this,' Jake replied, catching himself.

'Well thank you, for not calling me old.'

'You're welcome.'

The tea light between them flickered.

'So, given the limited time we have, can I ask you something personal?'

'You can ask,' said Jake, taking a sip.

'How many sexual partners have you had?'

Jake nearly choked on his virgin coke.

'You know if I answer then I can ask the same question?'

'Oh yes, sorry best not to answer then. I didn't think that one through, new to this. Shame I've been waiting to ask you that all evening, ever since they combined the groups.'

Jake mopped up a little spilt drink with a serviette.

'So what should we talk about?'

'Oh our hopes, our dreams,' Jake said with a mock flourish.

At a neighbouring table a couple were gushing over shared dog photos.

'Be honest, really, do you think I'm too old for this?'

'You're fine, you're lovely. You take care of yourself. You've still got it in you.'

'Thank you, it's nice to hear. You scrub up well yourself.'

The bell trilled again.

'Thank you, ladies and gentlemen. Please mark your cards and hand them in on the way out. We'll let you know your matches tomorrow.'

'So Janice, back to mine for some *Netflix and Chill*?'

'I'm not too old to know what that means, and that, is not, appropriate.'

'Yeah, sorry Mum.'

THE INCONVENIENT ALIBI

1

'That was the chief. The family of the victim are making his life hell and he's run out of patience, we're ordered to make that arrest.'

'So they want a conviction, and they think Stafford will do. What are you thinking?'

'Doesn't matter what I think. There's evidence. It's suspect evidence, but it does put him at the scene.'

* * *

'Good evening Mr Stafford, us again. I'm afraid this time we're charging you and taking you in.'

'Okay. Do what you've gotta do.'

'Strictly off the record, I'm hoping you beat the charges.'

'That's very understanding of you.'

Mr Stafford reached for his coat, hanging on a peg in his hallway.

'Do you need time to get anything together?'

'It's all here,' he said raising a leather bag that had been resting at his feet, 'I've been expecting this for a while.'

2

'Morning officers, forensics have finished. You can take a look.'

The man's body was crumpled on the cinder path, twisted and awkward. His cold blue eyes had not yet been closed, and stared up unseeing into the sky. His blue running top was soaked in a swamp of blackened blood, and there was a wound over his heart.

'Morning Chief, what have we got?'

'Forensics are saying a blow to the back of the head and stabbed by a serrated knife in the chest, most likely in that order. Dog units are searching the immediate vicinity.'

'Who's the victim?'

'Matthew Brady. Local, clean record, semi-retired author, lives just down there,' he said, pointing through the trees where the road curved and dropped down the hill into the town.

'Fully retired, it would seem.'

3

'Mr Stafford has asked me to convey his thanks to everyone for their support, which has been a great comfort at this difficult time. Mr Stafford will not be appealing the court's decision.'

'Alexa Morgan, *Tribune* – what do you say to reports that the evidence was planted?'

'Unfortunately Miss Morgan, while we believe that to be true, in fact the only explanation, there's no way to prove it.'

'Christie Dunn, *Gazette* – can you tell us why Mr Stafford won't be appealing?'

'I can't tell you, because he hasn't said. It may be the thought of another protracted court hearing, without compelling evidence of his innocence . . . and the sooner he starts his sentence the sooner he finishes it.'

4

'We've had a call, a dog-walker has found a knife, near where they found Brady. We'd better get over there. Could be the knife that killed him.'

'But that area was searched thoroughly - highly trained police dogs.'

'I know. Dogs don't make mistakes. They would have found it.'

'Well let's get over there and see this knife, maybe there's something incriminating still on it.'

5

'So what can you tell us, did you get a match on the blood?'

'Oh it's the one. The blood matches the victim. And there's a good set of fingerprints on the knife. But, the fingerprints are in the wrong place for a stabbing. There's a clear thumb print on the handle and a partial print on the ridge, indicating the knife was held like so, as you would to cut meat, or chop vegetables. It would be almost impossible to stab someone with sufficient force holding the knife like that.'

'Do we have a match for the fingerprints?'

'We do. It's a 95 per cent match, elimination prints taken from a burglary, only six weeks ago. A Thomas Stafford, 50 years old, local, no priors.'

'Let's go see if he's at home.'

6

'Mr Stafford?'

'Yes?'

'Officers Wilson and Rogers. My badge, his badge. We'd like you to accompany us to the station to answer a few questions.'

'Oh, what's this about?'

'There's been a murder. We believe you may be able to help us with our enquiries.'

'Okay. Hold on. I just need to lock up and set the alarm. It's new, so please bear with me. We had an intruder not long ago and I don't want to risk inviting him in again.'

'You said 'we' – do you need to call anyone?'

'Sorry, force of habit. I lost my partner a year ago. I still think of this as our place.'

'Sorry to hear it.'

'No need, but thank you.'

* * *

'We let him go home, there's nothing there.'

'He's not your killer?'

'No chief. I don't believe he is. We've been around long enough to know when a man has it in him, and this man does not, have it in him.'

'And the knife, with his fingerprints?'

'The knife was taken from his house, during a burglary, six weeks ago.'

'Well, don't give up too quick, it's him or back to square one,'

'It looks like an unlucky coincidence. His prints were taken for elimination after the burglary, otherwise he wouldn't be on the system. He's clean, just a few speeding tickets from twenty years ago.'

'In my experience, if something is too much of a coincidence then it's probably not a coincidence.'

'Okay Chief. We'll keep that in mind.'

7

Officer Wilson put a cup of coffee down on his partner's desk.

'What's new?' he asked.

'Oh, we're being crucified by the papers – did you see this front page? "Double widower framed – the evidence is obviously planted, the killer is still out there, and the police have given up".'

'*The Herald?*'

'Yeah, our *Friends of the Force.*'

'They're right though, I don't believe it was him.'

'While the evidence says otherwise.'

'There's something missing, something I can't put my finger on.'

'I know what you mean, it's keeping me up at night.'

'The knife has his fingerprints on. Fingerprints that don't match the method of killing. Blood that matches the victim. And no fingerprints in the blood.'

'A knife found three days after a thorough search with dogs, that Stafford admits matches one taken from his house in a burglary. If it was him, he could have dropped it into the Albany, or off Northshore Point, or practically anywhere. We do need to find the actual killer, not waste time investigating an old man who looks like he's being set up.'

Officer Wilson rubbed his eyes slowly.

'What evidence do we have in Stafford's favour?'

'None, just circumstances, and believability.'

'No motive, and no connection between the victim and the suspect.'

'None that we've found.'

'And an alibi, rather inconveniently.'

'A cleaner and security guard who both state he worked late as usual on the night of the murder, who would have noticed if he'd gone.'

Officer Wilson rubbed his eyes again and sighed.

'Read us your notes again on the alibi.'

Officer Rogers flipped through his notebook.

'Mr Stafford's alibi puts him in his office, working alone from 6 until 8 when he left for home. Mr Brady's time of death was around 7pm. The lab said there's only a thirty-minute margin of error. The site of the killing is ten minutes away from Stafford's office.

'The cleaner and security guard say Mr Stafford was in his office the whole time. Security Officer Donaldson says he can see most of Stafford's office from where he sits. He can't see where Stafford sits but he can see the lights going off and on when he takes a break, and the light from the photocopier, and he says Stafford was in there the whole time. Mrs Gonzales the cleaner also says she saw Stafford around 6 when he was talking to Donaldson at the entrance desk when she arrived, and again at 8 when he left through the main doors. So far no reason to doubt both of them.'

'And his car was in the car park, recorded on cctv the whole time.' Wilson added.

'The only cctv on the site, installed following a spate of recent thefts and vandalism.'

'So he left unobserved, in a different vehicle, drove over at just the right time for Brady to be out for his run, around the curve just out of sight of the houses, whacked him, stabbed him, drove back, left the car, and left the knife in the car or carried it around with him. He gets back in the building without being seen, without being missed, finishes up, waves everyone good-bye and drives home, as seen on cctv. He holds onto the knife for a couple of days only to absent-mindedly drop it near the crime scene, where someone will eventually find it. Totally illogical.'

'All under the noses of the security guard and the cleaner, who could at any point have knocked on his door and found him missing. That's too much of a risk.'

'They didn't watch him. They just thought he was there, because he hadn't left. Because his car was still there, he was still there.'

'No motive, limited means, a narrow and risky window of opportunity.'

'But evidence putting him at the scene of the crime.'

'Or ...' proposed Rogers.

'Or . . . the actual killer breaks in and fakes the robbery at Stafford's place. He knows Stafford's fingerprints will end up on file. And he finds something, something that has Stafford's fin-gerprints on, the knife being perfect. That was the motive for the break in. To find a fingerprint to leave at the scene.'

'But he didn't leave it at the scene, why wait and come back days later?'

'Maybe he was disturbed?'

'No witnesses have come forward.'

'And we have no clues as to who he might be and why he targeted Stafford . . .'

'A man with no enemies, just a regular law-abiding citizen so, no motive.'

The conversation had hit another dead end. Both men were tired of this case that refused to crack.

'And Mr Stafford himself?' asked Rogers.

'I like him. He's a little worn-down, but he seems resilient, warm-hearted. He's liked by his colleagues, especially the blue collars. And he's had it tough. First wife died young, cancer. Second wife-to-be died a year ago. Long-term relationship – four years. Killed when a drunk driver forced her and Mr Stafford off the road. She died at the scene. It was down in the canyon. No cameras, no dash-cam, no conviction.'

'That's tough to deal with. And then this happens.'

8

The packed courtroom hushed as the judge took his place and addressed the packed room. After the usual preamble he got to the point of business everyone was waiting for.

'Chairman of the Jury, how do you find Thomas Stafford?'

'Guilty.'

The court room exploded in uproar.

'Order! Order! – or we can clear the room and finish this without you! Order! Order!'

The volume dropped to indignant whispers and creaking seats as the gallery and floor resumed their seats, if not their composure.

'Thomas Stafford, for the murder of Matthew Brady, you are sentenced to five years. You will be eligible to apply for parole halfway through your sentence. Your sentence will include the time already spent in custody.'

Thomas Stafford just nodded and was escorted back to the cells, without a word.

'Good evening sir, we received a report of a robbery at this property.'

'Yes, thank you officer. Someone's been in here and they've turned the place upside down. Come in.'

'Any idea how they got in? Have you moved or touched anything?'

'I've tried not to touch anything. I think the porthole window in the cloakroom might have been open. Well it is now. It's too small to climb through so we don't bother closing it a lot of the time. That's not going to look good to the insurance company,'

'No, they don't take too kindly to paying out for open windows. If the burglary was for drug money, some of them addicts are awfully skinny. We'll check for fingerprints, and we'll take yours too, for elimination purposes.'

'It's such a mess. What were they looking for? I really don't have anything worth stealing.'

'Just looking probably, they see an open window or door and try their luck. Anything they can sell for cash.'

* * *

'Okay I'm done, I've taken some prints and we'll see if there's a match. Hopefully they won't all be yours. No footprints by your window I'm afraid. You can put everything back in place now. Have you found anything's gone missing?'

'Only the coins I had in this key bowl, loose change, and a kitchen knife that's missing from the rack.'

'Maybe he heard you coming in and grabbed the knife.'

'Really? He was here when I arrived, armed with my knife?'

'Maybe, well you scared him off without having to confront him, and before he could find whatever he thought you might have. So maybe you've had a lucky escape. Despite the mess. I'm done here for now. Here's my card, I'll be in touch. Keep that window shut. And get yourself an intruder alarm.'

'Yes sir, will do. Thank you Officer.'

'Mr Donaldson, did you see Mr Stafford leave the building, before 8pm on the night in question?'

'No sir I did not.'

'But he could have?'

'Yes, he could have. Not sure how he would have got back in though.'

'And he knew you could be checking rooms and keeping an eye on him that night, just like every other night?'

'Yes I guess he did. I'm not there to keep an eye on him though. I'm there to protect and secure the building.'

'Yes, quite. So if he had left the building there was every chance that you would find his room empty before he got back?'

'Yes sir.'

'And you didn't.'

'No sir.'

'And did you check his room on the night in question.'

'No sir, there was no reason to.'

'And who else was in the building that evening?'

'Just me and Rosita, Rosita Gonzalez, a cleaning lady.'

Mr Donaldson took a gulp of water. It was very hot on the witness stand.

'When was the last time you saw Mr Stafford prior to him leaving at 8 p.m.?'

'He came down from his office at around a quarter to six for a chat, to make sure I wasn't lonely he always said. As everyone had left early for the weekend. We always talk about football and soccer, films and whatever, he's a very interesting man, near photographic memory, useful to have on your quiz-team.'

'Quite, and was Mrs Gonzalez present at this conversation?'

'Well she starts at 6, so she came in while we were talking, said hello and talked for a bit until Mr Stafford went back to his office. Mr Stafford always had time for her, so if she saw him with me she'd always come over.'

'And when Mr Stafford left at 8 p.m. where was Mrs Gonzalez?'

'She was at the desk with me, she'd just finished – the cleaners' cupboards are next to the security desk. He waved goodbye to us on his way out.'

'He didn't come over?'

'No, we'd all already talked quite a bit earlier.'

'And did you notice anything odd about Mr Stafford, anything you can remember?'

'Nothing, nothing at all.'

'What time did Mrs Gonzales clean his office.'

'Ask her. She don't work for me.'

'Mr Donaldson, please answer the question. Remember you're not on trial here.'

'Sorry sir. No sir she didn't, she does the first floor on Fridays, he's on the ground floor.'

11

'As we discussed at the end of the last session, if you feel you are ready, maybe it's time for you to tell me about the night of the crash.'

'Oh, the crash, yes . . . it was terrible, doctor. This car came out of nowhere, ran us off the road. Didn't stop.'

'And with you was . . .'

'Kate, my girlfriend, my fiancée, was going to be my second wife . . . Lucy, my first wife, she passed away, cancer, horrible. I thought I'd never get over that . . . but time passes on. You can't live on memories . . . you have to live in the now as well. And Kate brought me out of the past and into the now, gave me my second chance.

'We were happy, we were good for each other, we'd given ourselves a new future.

'And then . . . and then it was gone. I watched her die, watched the light go out . . . I couldn't stop it. Her life just leaked out. And then she was dead.

'I felt like I had died too.'

'And then?'

'I sat in the car, unable to move. I might have stayed there all night if no one had come along. Someone stopped and called an ambulance, and the police arrived, and I was taken in for a check-up, but just scratches and bruises.'

'And did they find the driver.'

'No, they didn't. I was in shock, couldn't remember clearly for quite a while.'

'And the funeral?'

'Her family made all the arrangements. I couldn't do it.'

'I went. Not because I needed to be near her. Not to hear those beautiful eulogies. She wasn't there in that room, no matter what they said. I'd seen the life leave her body, gone. I went because I needed people around me, to lean on. My children, her children. My son came to live with me for a month, I couldn't bear to be alone. He stayed six months in all, until it got better, better enough to cope. Her family understood, gave me space, kept in touch.'

'And now?'

'We're all okay now. I know I was loved and am loved and that's all anyone can hope for. I'll see them both in the next life. I've dealt with it, now it's just a matter of time.'

12

The metal door clanged behind him and he made his way slowly to the car park, eyes wincing at the low sun.

'Officer Wilson, how good to see you – you haven't come to arrest me for another murder have you, I've only been free for a few minutes.'

'No no, you're okay.'

'I've served my time. I've paid my debt.'

'And you're free. No I just have a few loose ends.'

Stafford searched the officer's familiar face for clues.

'So, have you worked it out.'

'Mostly. You had me believing, I was on your side all the way through, that made it much harder.'

'Not just you. Everyone I care for, still cares for me, still believes.'

'You could have got away with it.'

'No one ever gets away with it, always there reminding you, eating you up, waiting to be caught.'

'Unless you serve your time.'

'Which I believe I have. Thank you for believing in me. In its own way that kept me going.'

'You traced the car to Mr Brady?'

Thomas Stafford shook his head in disagreement.

'Justice has been done, case closed.'

'Don't worry. No one out there believes you did it, they all know you were set up.'

'So the killer is still out there?'

'Leaving you to return to your loving family, wronged but free. Our mistake was to presume Brady's killer didn't want to be caught.'

'I have an alibi.'

'Yes, the guard and the cleaner ... that night they just weren't paying attention. You knew how it was. And in their minds it couldn't have been you, which made it easy to stick to their story, rather than give up the truth.'

'You don't need to look any closer. There's nothing new to be gained. I've paid my time, don't let it make trouble for anyone else.'

Just then three cars pulled into the car park, festooned with balloons and ribbons, and honking their horns.

'Well, here's your welcome home party, taking you back to a normal life. Good luck Mr Stafford, I have no more questions.'

They shook hands firmly.

'And stay out of trouble.'

'Will do sir, good day to you.'

SEVEN DWARVES

He didn't look at her when he spoke. She didn't answer. My spoon dropped from the high chair. They negotiated wordlessly who would pick it up. Blessed are the peacemakers.

Now he was in love he found beauty in everything, unfortunately mostly in himself for being in love. If she caught him one more time 'admiring' someone else, the end.

The car started with a shudder, then died. The starter motor wheezed, but wouldn't cough. Not today, of all days. His plans lay crushed. The ring would have to wait.

She smelt like the memories of good times ahead of him, of faithfulness. At that moment he knew what he wanted, and that he'd have to grow up quickly.

With a jagged skyline in the distance, she cruised past fields of wild flowers and ripening wheat, down to the twinkling sea. Alas, I was asleep through it all.

The rain fell quenching his rage. He'd emptied both barrels and now they were filling with water. They'd both have a fever in the morning.

Her face was out of focus but memorably delicious. So this is what kissing was really like, hot and eager, and Oww! You bit me!

FANCY DRESS

Every year it's the same, every year the club party is fancy dress.
Everyone asks what's the theme, what's the joke, but it always ends up the same.
I go as the phantom of the opera, he goes as a president, the same one every time.

A full face mask for us both, and everyone else also always the same.
It's like we don't think about what to do until it's too late and here we are again,
dragging out last year's costume, which was last year's costume last year.
One girl comes as a princess, she still has the costume from her school play.
One lad comes as Sinatra, always in the tuxedo, slick hair, with the bow tie hanging undone, another as Travolta, white suit, black shirt, open.
And there's always some 80's Madonnas, all black and dayglo and lace gloves.
And there'll be Blues Brothers, and Men In Black, and several Lara Crofts.

So this year me and he swapped costumes, took each other's, just to see how long we could get away with it.
The lights were lower and the dry ice was thicker and no one noticed at all.
So we vowed not to say a word, and see how long we could keep it going, before the trick was blown, and mingled.

When our girls turned up, fashionable late, they didn't seem to notice, and we being careful not to be heard, kept it going.
So I danced with his girl and he danced with mine, and we listened to what they said over the music, and nodded along.

His girl whispered to me, 'I can't wait to get you home. I can't. Let's find an empty room.'

I was firstly shocked at this offer, then not wanting to end this game quite yet gestured for her to 'hold on, be right back' and went to find the phantom.
I'd had an idea, a hope that actually the secret was out and she was playing along, to catch me out, to catch me good, and who would reveal first and where would it stop?

I found him on his own by the bar and pulled him into the hallway,
- So what goes, are you still being me?
- You are not going to believe this – I think I broke up with your girlfriend
- What?
I tore my mask off –
- Where is she, what did you say? Didn't she know it wasn't me – what were her words exactly?
- She said there was no point going on with this charade . . .

AFTER THE STORM

1.

A government spokesman read out the all-clear, unmistakable despite the poor signal. A voice that while neutrally informative had traces of relief around the edges. For a while after we sat staring at the radio, then looking at each other, seeking out eyes, making sure everyone had heard, silently unaware of what to do.

The tension was broken by cries from Sophie's baby, now awake and hungry or maybe celebrating what we daren't, somehow bringing us back to ourselves.

Tom and I climbed the concrete steps, pulled back the bolts and edged the bunker door open. A crack of light cut through the air. The counter still clicked but no faster than before. We all feared radiation but it was only light, illuminating a thin column of colour. We pushed the door open further, each scrape echoing wildly, and the brightness seemed to pour past, dimming its brilliance as it filled the room.

Everyone looked to me. I'd be the first out – not because I was brave, but because I needed to escape, and I needed to know, I needed some hope in what remained. I mentally checked my pockets and pack for essentials, and stepped out through the doorway.

There was no sound except the wind. The street was familiar, yet it was from another time, like a photo from a previous war, layered in grey. Broken windows, broken trees, roofs gaping open. No one around.

I made my way through the streets to where our house stood abandoned. I climbed through a broken window rather than try the front door. I don't know why, maybe to preserve crossing the threshold for another time. I picked my way through belongings, debris, grit and leaves that covered every surface, as if a hurricane had ripped through the house, pulling on everything that wasn't bolted down. In the kitchen I checked the electrics, gas cooker, and the taps, but nothing worked. Maybe the damage was superficial, repairable. There was nothing to collect, nothing useful, we'd taken all the supplies to the shelter in the days before the final warning.

And then I left, without checking upstairs or looking at your garden, sparing myself the sight, saving my memories a little longer.

I walked towards the bunker at the end of the next street through rubble and fallen trees. Some of the houses were only skeletons, possessions strewn as if carried out by a flood. Others had escaped with only broken windows, as if vandalised.

As I approached I could see the door was open a fraction. I wrapped my fingers around the edge and braced myself against the doorframe, scraping the metal door on the concrete floor until it was a quarter open. I stepped through the doorway and immediately turned and wretched, at the smell and sight that had greeted me, burnt emaciated bodies.

I waited until the nausea passed, took some sips of water from my bottle and before I knew it I was weeping. Weeping with grief and with relief, overlapping each other until I was done. Then I wrapped my scarf over my mouth and nose, put my reading glasses on to blur my eyesight, and pulled the door open to half way and turned on the fan just inside the door, to full speed. The counter was just inside the door too but the smell was too intense. I waited a couple of minutes outside for the stench to disperse, and went back in and checked the counter. The current reading was normal but the top reading marker had been pushed to the maximum.

My radio bleeped. It was Tom.

'The army are coming to take us to a safe place. We are advised to stay inside until evacuated. I have sent the return signal and we are scheduled for tomorrow morning. Please return before dark.'

'I hear you Tom, I'm turning back now. How's spirits?'

'Well, there's been some sobbing and some hugging. That's just me. No, it's everyone, it's just the relief. We're going to eat then a thanksgiving so get back soon. What's it like out there?'

'I'll tell you later, when we can't be overheard.'

'Now's good, I'm outside.'

'I don't know who made it, how many of us are left, it's a warzone out here. Bunker HA61 is ... err ... was ... it's a ... they didn't make it, massive radiation. I saw the readings, off the scale, looks like they couldn't get the vault shut in time.'

'May God have mercy on their souls. Are you coping?'

'I am, I had a moment, but it's passed.'

'Good, healthy. Anyone else about?'

'No one, but I haven't been far, and they'd have got the message to stay inside too.'

'Okay, see you soon, don't delay, over and out.'

Silence.

= = = = = =

2.

I still miss you. I am glad you didn't see this. Your compassionate heart, with your blunt objection to injustice, would not have coped. I have found your compassion in your absence, it's a comfort to know what you would have felt too. And I'm able to shut off unhelpful (healthy?) emotions and work on through when I need to, to carry those emotions unopened. Some later day an act of kindness (reminding me of you?) will open the locks for these emotions to equalise. I still miss you but I would not have wanted you to live through this. Your heart would have been broken or scarred. Neither could I bear to see. We are rebuilding what we need. We have some power and communications again. The World Service tell us the numbers. The cold war countries were best prepared, with their bunkers and bunker mentality. Other countries not so good. A minority survived in the capitals, where at least they had power and provision to rebuild. And those far from the capitals, where the situation had less reach were less affected.

We still don't know what happened, and I doubt we ever will.

We are growing our own food as much as possible, and animal breeding is a top priority, from those who remain and are healthy. Aid organisations are rebuilding as best they can, we all now belong to one. Seed repositories have been a godsend. Expertise is thinly spread. There's night classes on basic farming, mechanics, electrics and plumbing, and health, for everyone. We live in groups of four dozen, enough diversity to cover basic expertise while we catch up. Numbers are unreliable but between 5-25 per cent of populations survived. Heavy industry is suspended. It's reuse, repair, recycle as much as possible, no longer a green ideal but a necessity. We are slowly clearing areas and piling up anything useful, metal, cable, pipework, spare parts. This came true, but not how we wanted.

Sustainable power was less affected, particularly those sited in remote places. Nuclear power is suspended indefinitely. Power is gradually being restored and the grid fixed and allowances rising. I miss you.

I write this for you, knowing you can't see it, I know you aren't looking down, but sleeping, waiting for the day. I write this to keep you alive for me. Until we meet again, I still believe.